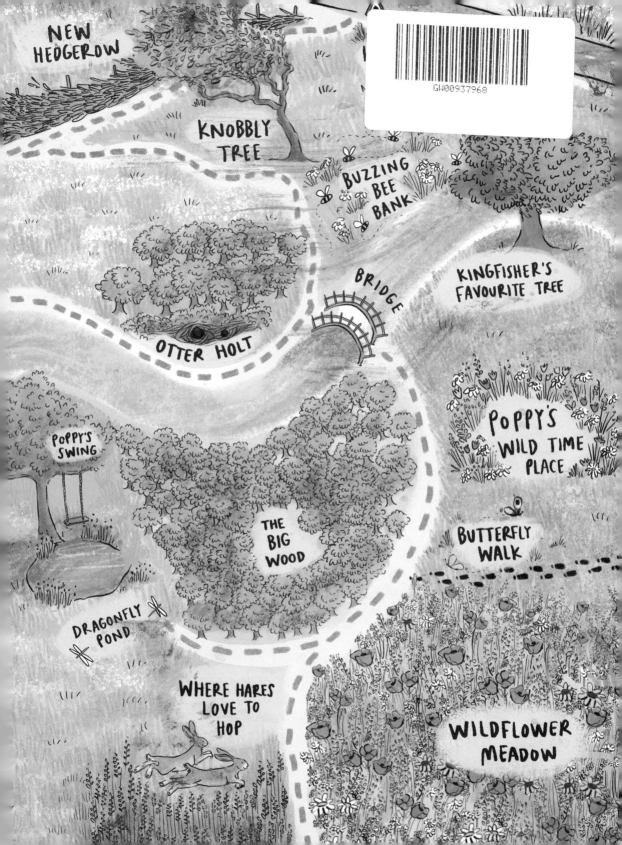

NEW HEDGEROW

KNOBBLY TREE

BUZZING BEE BANK

KINGFISHER'S FAVOURITE TREE

BRIDGE

OTTER HOLT

POPPY'S WILD TIME PLACE

POPPY'S SWING

THE BIG WOOD

BUTTERFLY WALK

DRAGONFLY POND

WHERE HARES LOVE TO HOP

WILDFLOWER MEADOW

POPPY
Goes Wild

Poppy Goes Wild *is a beautifully inspiring story wonderfully illustrated. To protect nature we must love nature and hear what our planet is telling us. This book serves as a reminder that we must also listen to our children. Out of the mouths of babes …*

Gordon Buchanan, wildlife cameraman and TV presenter

This enchanting book celebrates the thrilling experience of discovering wildlife when you are young. There are many lessons that we can learn from the past and allowing more land to run wild and free is a vital one.

Jimmy Doherty, food and nature TV presenter, and farmer

This is a cracking book. Poppy is cheeky and irresistible in her quest to make the world a better place for wildlife.

Iolo Williams, TV naturalist and Springwatch presenter

This charming tale is a timely reminder of the deep value in connecting more deeply with the natural world and allowing it to flourish and grow ever more wonderfully wild.

Olly Smith, *Mail on Sunday* wine columnist and broadcaster

POPPY
Goes Wild

WRITTEN BY
Nick Powell

Little
Steps

ILLUSTRATED BY
Becca Hall

Foreword

There is something exciting happening across our island. From city back gardens to urban parks, small farms to vast country estates, the natural world is being given a helping hand by people who truly care about it. They are creating safe havens to encourage the return of our native wildlife.

When I was growing up in Gloucestershire in the 1970s and '80s, the countryside seemed to me to be teeming with life, with hares hopping, hedgehogs snuffling, birds everywhere and a dazzling array of butterflies in flight. But in fact our wildlife was already under threat, as intensive farming and the industrial sprawl on the edges of our cities put delicately balanced habitats into devastating decline.

In the last three decades, many populations of insects, birds and small mammals, and the marine life around our coasts, have plunged to worrying levels.

But now there is a glimmer of hope. Trees are being planted, patches of land are being allowed to overgrow, and wild flowers are encouraged to spring up once more. People are beginning to understand that simply leaving spaces where nature can be allowed to perform its restorative magic can hugely enhance our gardens and our landscapes, and will entice many of these embattled creatures to return and flourish.

I urge you to be part of this 'rewilding' movement, in any way you can. Be like Poppy, in this charming and inspiring story. Get outside in the rain and the sun as often as you can. Get muddy and sweaty, look down at the ground and up into the trees, and peer into streams and ponds to see what you can see. Do all you can, as often as you can, to get as close to nature as you possibly can.

Wherever you live, see if you can create your own places to attract wildlife. Ask your parents to help you create a wild corner of your garden, or join a local nature club and find out what projects you can get involved with. Support your local Wildlife Trust, and visit the sites they are protecting and enhancing.

Check out the QR code at the end of this book to see a wide range of organisations. They can open the door to a whole host of wild adventures.

The reasons for doing these things are not just to benefit nature and repair the damage we have done. They are to help ourselves and enhance our lives. They remind us that we are part of nature; that when we harm the natural world, we hurt ourselves. But when we love nature and cherish and nurture it, and share its joys with our family and friends, we are looking after ourselves and our loved ones in the best possible way. We are in touch with that wild place in all of us that connects us to each other, and to every living thing.

Hugh Fearnley-Whittingstall

Chapter One

It was almost dawn and a perfectly plump red ball of sun was slowly peeping over the horizon, getting ready to bathe the farm in magical light. During the spring, when Poppy stayed at her grandad's farmhouse, she liked to leave a gap in the curtains, hoping that, as the sun rose, she would be woken up by her bedroom turning bright red.

Today the light was the reddest Poppy had ever seen. She decided it was a very good omen, as she had something very important she wanted to do.

Poppy loved waking up early at the farm, but she wasn't allowed to get out of bed until she heard the

sound of the first crow of the cockerel. Then she would race her grandad to see who could get to the kitchen first. Somehow she never lost, and today she was down at the kitchen table before the end of the cockerel's first cock-a-doodle-doo.

As her grandad came into the kitchen, Poppy unfolded her arms and started to unfold her thoughts very carefully.

'Morning. Now Grandad, I know you have told me what life was like on the farm when you were a boy, but I love hearing about it so much. Will you tell me again, please?'

'Of course I will. It was wild, Poppy, really wild!' replied her grandad. 'It was such a different place. It was full of wild flower meadows, and there were more wild fruits and more wild berries to pick than you could ever eat. There were huge hares that could bounce right over your head. There were skylarks that would soar higher and higher in the sky until you couldn't see them anymore, but you could still chase after them by following the sound of their beautiful song. At dusk, I used to hide outdoors, trying to spot a peregrine falcon dive-bombing at 200 miles per hour. But my favourite thing of all was watching the otters race each other in the river.'

'Well, guess what, Grandad? I have got a plan for us to make the farm full of all those amazing things again,' announced Poppy.

'Really? How are we going to do that, then?'

'We are going to turn the farm wild again!' said Poppy. 'Well, actually, we are going to "rewild" it. I have been reading about some of the farmers who are trying it. It sounds simple to me and it's a really important thing to do. You just have to stop doing all the things that destroyed the wild flowers and that forced the animals, birds and insects to leave. So that means stopping using pesticides, cleaning up the river and creating lots of overgrown, grassy areas for animals to feel safe enough to return to.'

'It sounds very interesting. How do you know so much about it?'

'Oh, I have my methods, Grandad.'

'I do like the idea, but it does sound like a lot of hard work.'

Poppy gave Grandad a very Poppy look.

Her grandad laughed. 'I know … hard work never hurt anyone.' It was one of his favourite sayings.

'I couldn't have put it better myself, Grandad. And don't worry, I am here to help. I will come every weekend and I will stay every day in the school holidays. And it only takes me half an hour to cycle from home, so I can be here whenever I am needed. It is going to be amazing! Don't you think?'

Her grandad couldn't quite believe what he was hearing. He seemed to be shaking his head in disbelief and nodding in agreement at the same time, but he grinned and said, 'Yes, Poppy, yes. What a great idea!'

Chapter Two

'Okay, Grandad, are you ready to go and find the areas that we are going to turn wild again?' asked Poppy.

'Yes! Let's go up to the field by the woods first,' replied her grandad.

'We are going to need some wooden stakes and some string, aren't we?'

'Exactly right, Poppy.'

When they arrived at the field, Poppy could see that it had been ploughed right up to the edge of the woods and that it was ready for sowing with crops. They planted the stakes into the ground, ten metres

away from the trees, and tied a line of string between them all.

They stood back to look at the long strip of land they had marked off, which was going to be free from crops from now on.

Poppy clapped her hands.

'When this is overgrown, the wild animals are going to love it, aren't they, Grandad?' she said.

'They will, Poppy, but to make it even more inviting I think we should plant some mustard and sunflower seeds here. And which bird do you think really loves eating the seeds as they fall off the flowers?' smiled her grandad, before raising his eyes to the sky.

His actions were a bit of a giveaway. He was talking about his favourite bird.

'Yes! The skylark!' whooped Poppy. 'I can't wait to see one soaring into the sky.'

'And soaring is just what they do, Poppy!'

'Ha, I think you may have told me that once or twice, Grandad.'

'But before we go and buy the seeds, I have just thought of something I should have shown you years ago,' her grandad said. 'Let's go into the woods over there, where there is still some long grass left. It's only a small patch because we dug up the rest, but it's been there since I was a little boy. So follow me as quietly as you can. And be patient!'

They went to the edge of the grass and Poppy's grandad pointed to his ear so that Poppy would listen very carefully. She wasn't sure, but there seemed to be a very faint squeaking sound. Grandad sat down and stayed very still, and Poppy copied him. Then he gently parted some long grass. Poppy held her breath. Just a metre away from her there were two little field mice, scampering around and gathering food. Poppy's eyes were as big as saucers as she watched them scurrying in the grass. She was surprised that the field mice hadn't rushed off straightaway and she even thought one of them had given her a little friendly glance.

It was the first time Poppy had really experienced a small creature close-up in the wild.

Poppy and her grandad immediately went out and bought the mustard and sunflower seeds. After they returned they scattered the seeds the full length of the area they had marked out, taking care to cover the seeds with soil, to make sure that the local crows didn't eat them before the plants had time to grow. They also staked out several more areas that they wanted to grow wild, including a long stretch along the riverbank.

Towards the end of the afternoon, they stopped at a large field.

'Poppy, I have been thinking. If we are going to do this properly, there can't be any half-measures,' Grandad said. 'This is the biggest field on the farm. I am going to stop growing crops on it and I am going to turn it back into a hay meadow. We will plant some wild flower seeds and hopefully before too long we should be knee-deep in swaying grass, with wild flowers popping up everywhere.'

'Brilliant, Grandad!' said Poppy. 'And if the research I have been doing is right, I think I know which animals will absolutely love that. Could it be the ones you used to watch bouncing around?'

'Bingo, Poppy! Spot on, the hares. It would be incredible for you to see just how high they can bounce. They adore eating the grass and flowers in hay meadows. But, most importantly, baby hares are born above ground, so the tall grass is also the perfect place for hares to safely conceal and raise their young.'

'Ha! Grandad, it really is beginning to feel just like I have got my very own David Attenborough,' laughed Poppy as they started on their way back to the farmhouse.

Whenever Poppy stayed at the farm, after they had finished the day's chores, her grandad allowed for an hour of what he called 'wild time', though he never quite knew what those words would mean to Poppy.

'Right, Grandad. Ready for some darts action?' asked Poppy.

Her grandad had been hoping that Poppy would forget about darts today, because this was darts with a difference. For her last birthday, he had made her a special hollow wooden blow-pipe and had given her

some rubber darts to fire from it. They had begun by firing darts at trees, and Poppy soon became a good shot. Today, she had a more ambitious plan to try out.

'Okay, Grandad, stay very still and try not to flinch!' she instructed, as she carefully balanced an apple on the top of his head.

Poppy walked back ten paces and put a dart into her blow-pipe. She took careful aim and drew in a long deep breath. *Remember, you have the cheeks of a bull-frog!* she said to herself.

Then she blew as hard as she could and, to her delight, the dart flew fast and true and knocked the apple flying off her grandad's head.

'Grandad, you flinched!' said Poppy as she ran over and gave him a high-five. 'Now that I have mastered the rubber darts, it won't be long before we try real arrows, will it?'

'Ha! We'll see,' he replied.

As they neared the farmhouse, the sun was settling down on the horizon, burnishing the fields and trees in a warm, gentle light. Poppy was convinced that the sun was staying up as long as it could to make the beauty of the evening last.

'Grandad, do you know one of the things that got me thinking about the idea of you turning the farm wild again? I learned that the words "otter", "lark" and "kingfisher" had been taken out of the *Junior Dictionary* that we use at school, because so many of those animals had disappeared from the countryside. I know how beautiful they all are, because you have told me lots of times. But most of my friends at school hadn't heard of any of them.'

'That is surprising!' her grandad replied. 'It makes me even happier that you came up with the idea of us trying to bring them back. When I was growing up on the farm, everyone talked about the word "progress" and about how important it was to grow as many crops as we could. We all thought we were doing the right thing, but now I can really see that we weren't being kind to nature at all.'

'Yeah, but at least you are now, Grandad!' she smiled, as they arrived back at the farmhouse.

Poppy gazed at the last reflections of red sunlight shimmering across the window panes. She started to think that something very special was taking place.

Chapter Three

At bedtime, Poppy's grandad always turned out her light and said, 'Goodnight Poppy, and remember: no reading under the covers.'

Poppy said goodnight and gave her grandad one of her special winks. She waited patiently until she heard the first snore from his bedroom. Then she got her phone out under the covers and continued the research that she had started on the internet. She was reading about what to do to encourage otters to return. If there was one animal she wanted to return the most, it was the otter.

Poppy and her grandad had already decided to

clean up the river and her grandad had stopped using pesticides, but she wanted to know what else needed to be done. As she was reading, she discovered that someone had built a riverside home for an otter and it had worked.

'Yes, that's it!' she shouted out loud. Luckily her grandad was snoring too loudly to hear her.

The next morning, the cock crowed and Poppy bombed downstairs, but somehow her grandad had beaten her to the kitchen. He must have bent the rules, but before she had a chance to quiz him, he said, 'Right. I have a new plan for how to get the otters back!'

'So have I!'

'Really? That's amazing. What a coincidence!'

'Yes it is, but you go first, Grandad!'

'Okay. I have been thinking that one of the biggest mistakes we made when we created so much farming land was straightening the lovely, winding river and draining off the wetlands,' her grandad explained. 'Those wetlands were home to an amazing mix of wild flowers, birds and all kinds of small mammals. By straightening the river, we lost the natural flood-plains and now, with climate change causing more rain, we can't do anything to stop the river flooding every year. So we have actually ended up with a smaller dry farming area, as well as less wildlife.'

'Mum said that if you can't sort the flooding out, you may have to sell up and move into a retirement home. Is that right, Grandad?'

'Well, we will just have to see how things go, Poppy, but I am not planning on going anywhere. And if we go ahead with my plan, I think we can stop the flooding and make the river area more appealing to otters again.'

'So, what *is* the plan?' asked Poppy.

'We need to go and destroy the deep artificial riverbanks so that the water can start flowing naturally again. It will create different habitats, and it will give life to lots of plants and animals and fish. Also, when the otters were still here, they never liked how dangerous the new deep, fast-flowing river became. The new river plain will give them plenty of little sandy banks and resting areas, with lots more places to find food to eat.'

'Wow, that sounds brilliant. I love destroying things!' said Poppy.

'And I have got just the thing. So follow me!' he replied.

It was still barely light as Grandad led the way to the barn. Once they were inside, he pulled away a tarpaulin to reveal an old red 1950s tractor. Poppy had never seen it before.

'We can attach a digger to my old tractor and use it to tear down the banks, Poppy. It will be just like

the old days on the farm when I was growing up.'

'I can't believe you've been keeping this tractor a secret, Grandad. I love it!' said Poppy, leaping on board.

Grandad tried to start the engine, and miraculously it worked the first time.

The old tractor seemed to love being in action again as it started removing sections of the steep banks. Grandad's reversing skills were really put to the test: they had to move very quickly as the water from the river started to pour out across one of the fields.

After a few hours of skilful digger work they had opened up the riverbanks in two important places, and retreated to admire their work.

'Ha, now I know why it's called a "wet" land!' said Poppy as she watched a new wetland being instantly created in front of her eyes.

'Just you wait, Poppy. All kinds of birds will see

the water from the skies and hopefully they will soon start coming back to splash around and feed.'

Poppy crossed her fingers at her grandad and he crossed his fingers back. It was the sign they now made to each other every time they had a good feeling about wild creatures returning to the farm.

They worked very hard reshaping a section of the river plain for the next week. Then it was time to put Poppy's plan into action.

'Okay, Grandad, I have read that in order to try and ensure the return of otters, some farmers and conservationists have been creating homes for them out of fallen branches. They are called holts..'

'Great idea! Maybe the internet isn't such a bad thing after all. You're becoming quite the expert, aren't you,' chuckled her grandad.

'Hop on again,' he continued. 'I know where to find some branches to drag down to the riverbank. It seems funny now but my dad used to let me drive the tractor on my own when I was only nine.'

But before he could finish speaking, Poppy had elbowed him out the way and was sitting behind the steering wheel.

'What a great idea, Grandad! In case you haven't realised, that means I am old enough to drive. So let's go!'

'H-h-hold on a second, Poppy!' Grandad stuttered.

'Ha! No, *you* hold on, Grandad. What was good for you must be good for me!' Giving her most impish grin, Poppy floored the accelerator and off they went, lurching across the fields. Her grandad had to hold on so tight that he didn't notice his hat flying off.

But Poppy could see that he was soon secretly enjoying the bumpy ride as his face settled back into its special grandad smile. With Poppy at the wheel, it took ages for the tractor to drag enough branches to the riverbank, but finally they had a huge pile.

They started to make the holt by laying branches on top of each other in a crisscross pattern, and before they finished they carefully checked that they had left enough of a gap at the bottom for the otters to enter.

'Otters need somewhere to sleep for hours at a time because they use so much energy catching fish at night. And they need to feel safe during the day when humans and other animals are out and about,' puffed an exhausted Grandad, sitting back against his old tractor.

'This should work a treat then!' said Poppy. 'Right, what's next?'

'Poppy, there is so much to do that I think I need a cup of tea before I carry on.'

What is it with grown-ups and cups of tea? thought Poppy, but she didn't complain because she could see her grandad was exhausted.

'Okay … but I think we're going to need some help!' she said.

Chapter Four

When she wasn't staying at her grandad's farm, Poppy lived in the nearby town. Her classmates spent most of their time in the town, but she was hoping that they would help her to return wildlife to the countryside. It was the middle of the holidays, so she visited all her classmates and asked them to get involved in cleaning up the river.

She was thrilled that so many of them wanted to help. The river on the farm stretched over a mile so it was going to be hard clearing out all the rubbish, and removing all the plastic bottles and bags that they could find for recycling.

Poppy's friends stuck to their task and worked on clearing the river regularly over the next few months, as autumn arrived and then turned to winter. The headteacher at their school was impressed.

Poppy had also worked out that the water that flowed through the town needed to be cleaner by the time it arrived at the farm, so when she asked her headteacher if the whole school could get involved in clearing up the river in the town too, he immediately said yes.

While the clearing up was going on, Poppy and her grandad continued to work on the riverbanks, through summer and into the following spring, returning the river to its natural meandering course across the river plain. Poppy had lost count of how many times they had been up and down the river in the tractor, moving piles of mud.

'I love mud, Grandad!' said Poppy. 'And I really love how the river is different now. There already seem to be a lot more birds too.'

'The river level is so much shallower, just as it is meant to be. Hopefully we will get some rare water-loving birds back soon. And do you know something else, Poppy? It's already the last week of March. The worst of the rains have gone, and this is the first time the river hasn't flooded for ten years!'

'I was keeping my fingers crossed about the flooding, but I didn't want to say anything in case I jinxed it!' smiled Poppy.

The rest of the plan seemed to be starting to work too. No pesticides had been used on any of the crops for a year, and in just a few places, for the first time in decades, the riverbed was becoming visible again.

During the remaining part of spring, the landscape on the rest of the farm changed dramatically too. The new wild, grassy areas were looking deep and dense, ready to invite the return of the wildlife that had been absent for so long.

Then, as early summer arrived, the time came for Poppy and her grandad to discover how successful their efforts so far had been.

It was early June, and Poppy's mum dropped her at the farmhouse with everything she needed for a long stay. Poppy had put in lots of miles cycling to and from her grandad's and now she was super fit. Her mum had agreed that she could stay at the farm for the last few weeks of the summer term, as long as she promised to arrive at school on time every day.

'Right, Poppy,' said Grandad, 'you have arrived at a very good time. Now follow me. We are going off to the big field. Nature has been working away, so as we walk, keep your eyes, ears and nostrils alert.'

As they strolled past the new clumpy, overgrown areas of grass, brambles and dandelions, Poppy said, 'It sounds incredible. It's really much noisier than before. I can hear a bee buzzing every few seconds. But what's that kind of rattling sound?'

'Ah, yes,' Grandad replied. 'That's the grasshoppers chirruping. They seem to be particularly excited to be back. Now, as we walk past the tiny pond next to the oak tree, see if you can hear a helicopter.'

Poppy gave him a quizzical look, but she was all ears as they approached the pond. Then, bang on cue, she started to hear what sounded like a mini helicopter coming closer … then suddenly a dashing turquoise dragonfly was hovering in front of her nose. Poppy was too entranced to say anything, but later she was convinced that the dragonfly had come to introduce himself.

Grandad, meanwhile, had that very contented smile on his face again.

'Come on, Poppy, there is so much more to see. We are almost at the big field we planted with wild flower seeds to make a hay meadow. When we get nearer, I will tell you when to close your eyes.'

Poppy followed his instructions, and as they arrived her grandad shuffled her into position. He tapped her on the shoulder and she opened her eyes.

The two-acre field was unrecognisable. It had been transformed into a knee-high meadow, with plants swaying gently in the breeze. Mingled within the sea of intensely bright green grass were the flickering yellow-gold of the meadow buttercups and the ox-eye daisies, and the truest, bluest of blues of the cornflower.

But the dazzling bright red of the dancing poppies caught Poppy's eye the most. She had never seen them growing wild before.

Not for the first time that day, she stayed quiet for a while. And then she said, 'Grandad, do you know, seeing the flowers bursting into colour gives me a tingly feeling in my tummy. And I have realised it makes me feel very happy.'

'I think it is because you are being kind to nature,' replied Grandad.

'So that means that being kind makes you happy,' said Poppy. 'I am going to remember that.'

'You do just that, Poppy. Now, I know we haven't done any hard work yet, but before we do, do you fancy a bit of "wild time" on the river?'

'Whoop!' came the reply and they headed straight for the river.

Sitting on the new shallow riverbank was a very rickety old raft. 'Grandad, is that what I think it is?' asked Poppy.

'Yes, it's my old raft. It hadn't been used for 50 years so it needed repairing, but it's ready for a spin.

'Now that's *really* wild!' said Poppy as she picked up the raft and took a flying leap into the river. She went hurtling downstream and for a moment she looked in control, until she hit the rapids and flew off the raft. She dragged herself to the bank while her grandad rescued the raft before it disappeared downstream.

'Wow, that was brilliant! Thank you, Grandad.'

'My pleasure, Poppy,' Grandad smiled. 'But if you are going to float on it to go looking for otters, like I did when I was a boy, you may have to take it a bit more steadily!'

Poppy got straight back on the raft to try again.

Over the next few days, perhaps the most common sight on the fast-changing farm was what looked like a runaway raft bobbing along on its own along the river. But if you looked carefully, from time to time you would see a girl's head pop up at one end of the raft, and a stray leg trying to wrap around it. Poppy

was spending more time under the raft than on top of it. It was a good job the river water was getting cleaner, because she couldn't help taking giant gulps of it.

The big question, though, was whether the water was becoming clean enough to attract the otters. Poppy was convinced that the groups of small silver fish that had appeared, shimmying in the sparkling sunlight alongside her raft, were a very positive sign.

Chapter Five

'Morning, Grandad. Hedgehogs?' asked Poppy.

'Yes, Poppy, there used to be lots of hedgehogs living here, especially in the hedgerows bordering the fields,' her grandad replied. 'The hedgerows provided the perfect home for them to feed on all the insects living there. They also allowed the hedgehogs to take shelter from predators like badgers.'

'I guess they're not called "hedge" hogs for nothing!' laughed Poppy.

'That's right, but I am afraid that we ripped the hedgerows out to create more farming land and to make it quicker to get around. I don't know exactly when, but eventually I stopped seeing hedgehogs.'

'I have been thinking, Grandad,' said Poppy, 'that it must be hard being a farmer because it's your job to grow enough for people to eat, which sometimes means the best decisions aren't made for wildlife.'

'That seems a fair way of putting it, Poppy, and as each day passes I become more convinced that an animal-friendly, wilder way of farming is the only way to go.'

'So, how do we get the hedgehogs back?'

'Well, I am hoping that very soon we will see hedgehogs coming to the wild fringes around the fields that we have created,' Grandad explained. 'Those edges are teeming with the juicy insects they love. But we also really need to put the hedgerows back in place. It is much harder than ripping them out though, so you will be glad to know that I began the first steps last winter when you were at school. Next, we have to do the fun bit.'

'Yes! You know I love surprises. And I have got a little one for you too. I have invited my classmates around to see what jobs they can do to help. And they should be arriving about … now!'

At which point there was a knock at the door.

'No time like the present!' said Poppy and her grandad at exactly the same time. It was another of his favourite sayings.

Restoring the hedgerows was going to be a long-term job, and some would need to be planted from scratch. But Poppy's grandad had started the process of creating a stretch of hedgerow, using a technique that had been around for centuries. Grandad had learned it as a boy.

Alongside one of the fields, there was a straggling line of low trees. Last winter, Grandad had begun by partly sawing through the thin trunks at the bases of the trees, before bending them over diagonally. Then he had left them to settle.

Now that late summer had arrived, there was no chance that any birds would be nesting among the bent branches. So, it was safe for Poppy and her classmates to start carefully weaving the leafy

branches together, filling in the gaps to create what
looked more like a hedgerow.

Next, they helped to gather hazel branches from
the nearby wood, which were then hammered into
the ground as stakes to provide extra support
for the hedgerow.

In just a few days, they managed to lay a long section that would soon start to really thicken. But even now it was an instant haven for hedgehogs.

Poppy and her grandad began spending more and more time down by the river, hoping to catch sight of any returning wildlife. He couldn't be completely sure, but one day Grandad thought he saw a flash of electric blue just above the water. And if he had, that could only mean one thing … the kingfisher was back. He almost didn't dare think about it, but if the kingfisher had returned, it was a very good sign that the otters may be close to returning too.

Poppy's rafting skills had now come a long way. So had her tractor driving. Her grandad had begun to enjoy being driven around, with Poppy doing some of the hard work.

Today, the long grass needed to be cut in the golden hay meadow. The wild flowers had dried out and it was time to cut them back, to allow the seeds to drop into the rich earth. That, in turn, would lead to even more wild flowers next year, and even more of the bees and butterflies that loved the flowers.

While Poppy was having a go at cutting the long meadow grass, out of the corner of her eye she thought she saw something leaping. But she was concentrating so hard on driving in a straight line she couldn't be sure. Then, as she turned the tractor off and jumped down, she was greeted by the most extraordinary sight.

Right in front of her were four hares who appeared to be taking it in turns to hop up and down. She knew they could hop, but she had never known how high. Then they raced around the field in pairs at incredible speed, before dashing right past Poppy and bouncing off into the woods.

She only just managed to say, 'I have never seen anything like this, Grandad … it's incredible!'
'I don't think many humans have, Poppy.'

'It's amazing that they're back, isn't it! It almost seemed like they were bouncing so close to say hello!'

'Well, in all my years, I have certainly never seen them do that,' said Grandad.

'I am not going to forget that for the rest of my life!' Poppy replied.

It was time to head back to the farmhouse. They had been driving the tractor quietly for a few minutes when Poppy asked, 'Grandad, what is that saying you have again about nature?'

'In nature, nothing tries to be perfect, because everything already is.'

'I think I get it now. It sort of means that knobbly bent tree just over there is beautiful just the way it is,' said Poppy.

'That's right, and it's a good way of looking at life too,' replied Grandad.

'I like that,' said Poppy. 'Though you know what will be really perfect? The moment we get back for your homemade elderflower cordial. I'm parched!'

'Ha, me too!' laughed Grandad, as Poppy put her foot down and they bumped their way home.

Chapter Six

One morning Poppy woke up really early, well before the sun was ready to warm her toes through the gap in the curtain. She jumped out of bed and peered from her window to see a winding ribbon of pure silver. The river was now flowing in perfect crescents on the new flood-plain, and there was a perfect crescent moon shining intensely in the clear pre-dawn sky. Poppy felt the river was calling to her.

She got dressed as quietly as she could and sneaked downstairs. Grandad and the cockerel were both still fast asleep. She was amazed at how still and quiet the farm seemed as she followed the silver moon all the

way down towards the riverbank.

'Good morning, raft. Are you ready?' she said on arrival. Though she wasn't quite sure why she had started talking to something made of wood.

She started to glide downstream and all she could hear was the water rippling around her raft. Then she heard another rippling sound, which sounded almost like an echo. Then she heard another one. And then, right alongside her, the head of an otter popped sleekly out of the water. The otter looked at

Poppy, cocked its head to one side and slipped under the water again.

In the half-light, Poppy wondered if she was imagining things.

The otter reappeared, floating backwards and overtaking her, then leap-frogging back and forth just ahead of the raft. It slowed down in front of her and Poppy thought it nodded to her. And then it was gone.

Poppy immediately steered to the bank and prepared to sprint off to tell her grandad. But she didn't need to. Grandad's sixth sense about that morning had kicked in too, and he was on the opposite side of the bank, pumping his arms in the air with a huge grin on his face.

They walked arm-in-arm back to the farmhouse. They were both talking so much that neither of them had a clue what the other was saying. In the kitchen, Grandad started cracking eggs and Poppy didn't even need to ask: today it was definitely going to be pancakes for breakfast.

Once she had worked her way through a sea of syrup, Poppy said, 'Grandad, I have been hoping so much that this day would come, and now that it has, I have got another plan I want to suggest.'

'Okay. I'm listening,' he replied.

'For years you have been having lots of money problems running the farm, haven't you?'

Grandad nodded.

'And I know it was made worse by the cost of all those years of flooding,' Poppy continued. 'Well, now that so many amazing animals and wild flowers are beginning to return, I am sure that people will be happy to pay to visit. And it's really important for people to see what we are doing here too, isn't it?'

'I think you may have a point there, Poppy.'

'I have read about some other farms doing that, so if you do it too and if visitors pay, you will be able to stay at the farm forever, and I will be able to come whenever I want to!'

'I am sure you're onto something, but maybe we still need some more creatures to return to attract enough visitors,' said her grandad. 'Let me have a little think.'

'Okay, Grandad,' she replied.

Poppy knew her grandad very well and she was pretty convinced his answer was going to be yes. But just in case he needed a little more persuading, she set out in the evening sunlight to see if she could spot any new returning creatures.

Grandad had told her how much he loved skylarks when he was growing up, and she was really hoping that she would be able to see one herself for the first time.

The previous year, Poppy and her grandad had

planted mustard and sunflower seeds on one edge of the woods, to help entice the skylarks back. When she arrived there, she heard the very satisfying sound of lots of seeds on the ground underneath her feet. *Perfect for skylarks to munch on,* she thought.

She looked straight up at the sky and waited … and waited. She gave her neck a rest and then waited some more. For a moment, she thought that she could see something tiny fluttering high above her. But skylarks can soar up to 100 metres from the ground, so she really couldn't be sure.

Poppy was a little disappointed, but if there was one thing she had learned recently it was that nature does its own thing in its own time. So her thoughts turned to the hedgehogs, and she went to check the new hedgerow they had recently made.

Poppy recalled her grandad's words of advice. 'Hedgehogs are pretty shy, so be very quiet and slow moving when you're looking for them,' Grandad had explained. 'You're far more likely to hear one before you see one, as they make quite a snuffling noise when they are nosing around for food. And when they're content, they make a happy, purring sound.'

She lay on the ground for ages but there was only silence. She was beginning to get a little frustrated, but then she remembered that her grandad had said that hedgehogs would also like the new overgrown areas they had created, which were crammed with insects.

She set off for one of the strips of land that she hadn't visited for a while. When she was about ten metres away, she knew she was in luck. The sound of purring filled the air. It was a very soothing sound and in a funny way it made Poppy feel a little sleepy. Then, as dusk approached, she heard a few excited squeaks and some noisy shuffling. Poppy crept closer and discovered six hedgehogs waking up before their evening forage. She was transfixed.

But then she felt a sudden panic and sprinted back to the farmhouse.

'You will never guess what, Grandad! I haven't just seen one hedgehog. I just saw *six* of them!'

'*Yes!*' boomed Grandad.

'But I am really worried because they are living on a strip of land right near the road. The drivers won't have a clue that the hedgehogs are there. We need the cars to slow down to protect them, so can we make some safe-crossing road signs for hedgehogs, please?'

'Now, that is a clever idea! I think I can rustle up some bits and pieces for the signs,' he replied.

The following day they searched Grandad's barn for what they needed. It took a little while. Grandad never threw *anything* away, but that always meant he had what was needed for any handy job. They loaded up the tractor, having worked out that three road signs should be enough.

While her grandad hammered the signs together,

SLOW

heDGEHOG

CROSSING

Poppy got to work with her paintbrush creating outlines of hedgehogs.

As the sun began to set, they stood back to take in their work.

'I am not sure that they really look like hedgehogs, do they?' asked Poppy.

'Oh I don't know. They look pretty hedghoggy to me,' grinned Grandad.

'I guess they should do the trick! Now come on, Grandad. Let me show you the hedgehogs before they go off on their night-time search for food.'

Chapter Seven

'Poppy, come outside for a second, will you?'
Grandad called.

As she walked out of the back door, Poppy was
handed a pair of binoculars.

'Look over in that direction, where we planted the
mustard and sunflower seeds. And tell me if you can
see anything,' said Grandad.

The word 'seeds' made Poppy's heart start to race.

'Grandad, I can't hold the binoculars still! I am
shaking too much!'

'Okay, put them down for a minute,' her grandad
smiled. 'Now listen very, very carefully. Ignore the

immediate sounds around you, and try to see if you can hear anything in the distance.'

A few seconds later, a look of amazement appeared on her face. Grandad smiled and nodded. Poppy raced away from the farmhouse, with her wellies just about managing to keep up with her. She ran and ran, getting closer and closer to the most beautiful bird-song she had ever heard. Eventually she stopped to see a skylark hovering only about ten metres off the ground. She could even see the tufty feathers on top of its head.

Poppy thought that the skylark seemed to be waiting for something. Just at that moment, Grandad arrived on his tractor. He got down and stood next to Poppy. The skylark started to flap its wings even faster and sing even more like an angel, and then it set off, spiralling towards the sun. Poppy watched the skylark become a tiny speck, as it flew upwards and eventually disappeared from sight.

'Wow!' said Poppy.

'Wow!' said Grandad.

After a long pause, Poppy said, 'That was incredible, wasn't it, Grandad? I think we may be ready for visitors to come now, don't you?'

'How could we not, Poppy, how could we not?' he replied.

There were lots of preparations to be done before visitors could be invited to the farm. Simple maps were drawn up and route signs were put in place, so that the visitors could get the most of their visit. It took quite a few attempts, but eventually Poppy was happy with the spot-the-creature guides she had made for the children.

Before long, the big opening day arrived.

It was a perfect afternoon and the river was swarming with life. There seemed to be people

everywhere, strolling along the riverbanks and the
wetland areas, taking in the dazzling array of wild
flowers and bulrushes.

There were more visitors than Poppy could ever have hoped for. Some of the children busied themselves spotting the frogs bouncing around the lilies. Others sprinted after the damselflies darting to and fro, but they didn't stand a chance of keeping up with them.

'Grandad, have you noticed that all the adults are smiling as they look around, but none of them seem to be saying much?' asked Poppy.

'I have, yes. And I think we know that feeling quite well too, don't we?'

'We do,' Poppy agreed. 'But it looks like the adults may have travelled back in time to a forgotten place.'

'That's a little deep but I think you're right.'

'Also, I know I have kind of said it before, and maybe I shouldn't say this out loud, but I am pretty sure that when every creature has first returned to the farm, it has given me a special look. I think that they must know what we've been doing to turn the farm wild again,' wondered Poppy.

'Wouldn't that be amazing if it were true!' Grandad replied.

The late afternoon sun was showing the river off at its sparkling best. It was somewhere between silver and gold, and was like a magnet to the families sitting along the banks, enjoying their picnics.

Suddenly people started pointing to the river. Gasps of appreciation seemed to be rippling along the riverbank.

Right in the middle of the river, three otters were dipping and diving together, and hurtling along at high speed.

They seemed to be taking it in turns to surge out of the water to show how graceful they were. They flowed just under the surface like torpedoes and somehow they were able to move at exactly the same speed. Poppy thought it looked like they were racing, but whatever they were doing they were putting on an incredible show.

Once the otters had reached the end of the stretch of the river on the farm, they popped out on to one of the muddy banks. They shook themselves dry and looked back at the line of people on the riverbank. Then they seemed to look directly at Poppy and her grandad.

'Did they really just give us a little nod?' asked Grandad.

Poppy was sure they had. Then the otters dived back into the river and swam away downstream.

The visitors broke into spontaneous applause. The sound of chattering didn't stop until long after they had left the riverbank. Nobody could ever have expected to see something so special.

As the sun went down it began to feel very peaceful and quiet. Poppy and her grandad were sitting, content and exhausted, basking in the golden light

reflecting off the river. They thought they were alone until Grandad pointed at three familiar faces who had returned to enjoy the sun.

'Thank you, otters,' beamed Poppy. 'Grandad, it's so beautiful here, and it almost feels like too much for us to take care of, but I'm never going to stop trying.'

'Me too, Poppy. There are so many creatures that I want to see returning to the farm.'

'I have got a list. Have you?' she asked.

'Yes, I have.'

'Let's take it in turns to say one thing we hope to see on the farm!' she suggested.

'Okay, you start, Poppy.'

'A beaver building a dam,' said Poppy, mimicking a beaver gnashing its teeth.

'Barn owls hooting,' said Grandad, hooting like an owl.

'A peregrine falcon dive-bombing,' offered Poppy,

swooping like a bird.

'The coo of a pair of turtle doves,' cooed Grandad.

'Bats screeching,' squealed Poppy.

'The song of a nightingale,' Grandad twittered.

'A bull-frog doing big stinky burps!' burped Poppy.

The list went on and on and on … until Poppy said, 'Grandad, there is something else I would love to do. We should put on a Halloween Scare Night for visitors. We will have freaky hay-bale rides, screeching bats, howling foxes, eerie owls and slithering snakes … and that's just for starters!'

As they strolled back to the farmhouse, one thing was for sure: Poppy and her grandad had already achieved a lot in starting to turn the farm wild again, but their mission to make the world a better place for wildlife had only just begun.

About the Author

Nick is a multi-award winning television producer whose many credits include launching the series *Supernanny*, *Escape to River Cottage*, *Nigella Bites*, *Food Unwrapped* and *Blood, Sweat and T-Shirts*.

Born and raised in the Black Country, Nick grew up with a strong appreciation of the rivers, wild meadows and rolling hills of the surrounding countryside. As a teenager he was transfixed by the magical sight of an otter catching a fish and sunning itself on the riverbank. He didn't see another one in the wild until decades later, when our rivers began to be cleaned up.

He is now lucky enough to divide his time between living alongside the South Downs National Park and the wild-flower meadows of the French Alps.

About the Illustrator

Becca is a freelance illustrator originally from the Lake District, now living in Cornwall. She studied illustration in Manchester and, since graduating, she has worked on a variety of children's books and other projects, as well as launching her own range of homewares and gifts. She loves to draw and paint by hand.

Discovering nature is a theme that Becca is especially excited about. As a child, her grandparents let her explore and play in their woodland in the Langdales, where she made dens from broken branches and little gardens for the hedgehogs from moss and leaves, all while watching deer and badgers rustle about.

For my nippers, Martha, Elsa and Dexter ...
live wild and free ~ NP

For GG and her wildflower meadow ~ BH

For more information about getting involved, scan the code.

First published in the UK in 2020
Published in paperback in the UK in 2021
by Little Steps Publishing
Uncommon, 126 New King's Rd, London SW6 4LZ
www.littlestepspublishing.co.uk

ISBN: 978-1-912678-26-6 (HB)
ISBN: 978-1-912678-28-0 (PB)

A CIP catalogue record for this book is available from the British Library.

Designed by Verity Clark

Printed in China
1 3 5 7 9 10 8 6 4 2